THE·FAIR·AT·KANTA

THE·FAIR AT·KANTA

·A·STORY·FROM·PERÚ·
·by·Carlos Antonio·Llerena

·HOLT·RINEHART & WINSTON·
NEW·YORK

PUBLISHED SIMULTANEOUSLY IN CANADA BY HOLT, RINEHART AND WINSTON OF CANADA, LIMITED.

DESIGN & CALLIGRAPHY BY CARLOS·ANTONIO LLERENA
PRINTED IN THE UNITED STATES OF AMERICA
FIRST EDITION
654321

LIBRARY OF CONGRESS CATALOGING IN PUBLICATION DATA·
LLERENA, CARLOS ANTONIO
·THE FAIR AT KANTA·

SUMMARY: A YOUNG PERUVIAN BOY LIVING IN THE ANDES WITH HIS GRANDMOTHER TAKES HIS FIRST HARVEST TO MARKET WITH THE AID OF A MAGIC FLUTE.
(I. PERU· SOCIAL LIFE AND CUSTOMS·FICTION.
2. MAGIC· FICTION) I. TITLE.

PZ7. L767Fai   (E)   74.6764   ISBN 0·03·014766·2

 CON TODO MÍ CORAZÓN PARA :
Eduardo LLerena·Susana Aguirre LL·
IN MEMORY of the EARTHQUAKE
VICTIMS, PERU 1 9 7 1
To Miriam Chaikin

PAUCAR'S MOTHER AND FATHER WERE KILLED IN AN EARTHQUAKE. HE LIVED WITH GRANDMOTHER ON THE PUNA, THE VERY HIGHEST PART OF THE ANDES MOUNTAINS.

PAUCAR FARMED THE LAND, PLANTING BARLEY. HE CALLED THE LAND MAMA PACHA, WHICH IN QUECHUA, THE INCA LANGUAGE, MEANS MOTHER EARTH. IN THE SPRING, WHEN THE BARLEY TURNED GOLDEN, HE WOULD TAKE IT TO THE FAIR AT KANTA AND EXCHANGE IT FOR OTHER PRODUCTS. PAUCAR LONGED FOR THAT DAY.

GRANDMOTHER OFTEN TOLD PAUCAR STORIES ABOUT THE TIME OF THE INCAS, WHEN PERU WAS A GLORIOUS NATION, UNTIL THE SPANISH CONQUERORS CAME.

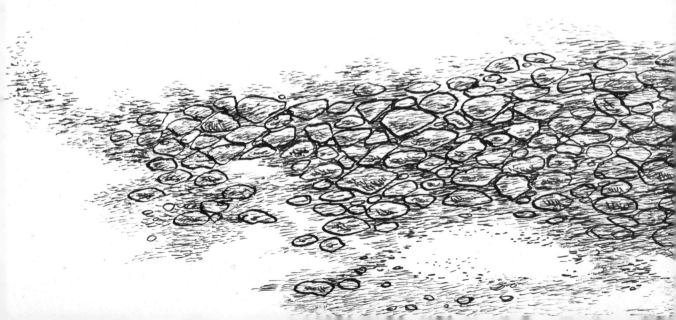

AS THE LLAMAS GRAZED HE
WOULD PLAY HIS QUENA AND
LISTEN TO ITS SWEET TONES
ECHO BACK FROM THE MOUNTAINS.

At last it was time to take the barley to Kanta. Paucar filled 20 sacks with beautiful golden barley and tied them to the llamas. Grandmother gave him a flute to play only in case of danger, and he set out on his way.

PAUCAR WALKED ALL DAY. HE TOOK SHELTER FOR THE NIGHT IN A CAVE. HE UNTIED THE SACKS, SO THE LLAMAS COULD REST, AND PUT THE BARLEY IN A DRY CORNER. THEN HE ATE AND WENT TO SLEEP.

AN OLD FOX OUT HUNTING
CAME UPON THE CAVE AND
STOLE THE 20 ROPES.

WHEN PAUCAR AWOKE, HE FOUND THE ROPES GONE. HE STARTED TO CRY. WITHOUT ROPES, HOW COULD HE GET HIS BARLEY TO KANTA? THEN HE REMEMBERED THE QUENA GRANDMOTHER HAD GIVEN HIM, AND HE BEGAN TO PLAY.

SUDDENLY, A DUSTY OLD DONKEY APPEARED AND SPOKE TO THE LLAMAS.

"DEAR SISTERS, WHY IS YOUR MASTER SO SAD?" THE DONKEY SAID.

"LAST NIGHT SOMEONE STOLE HIS ROPES. NOW HE CAN'T TAKE HIS BARLEY TO THE FAIR," THE LLAMAS ANSWERED.

"IT WAS THE OLD FOX WHO TOOK THEM," THE DONKEY SAID.

HOW SURPRISED PAUCAR WAS!! HE HAD UNDERSTOOD EVERYTHING THAT THE ANIMALS HAD SAID. PAUCAR SILENTLY THANKED GRANDMOTHER FOR THE MAGIC QUENA.

"DEAR BROTHER," HE SAID TO THE DONKEY, "HELP ME GET MY ROPES BACK AND I'LL GIVE YOU 3 SACKS OF BARLEY."

THE DONKEY AGREED. TOGETHER, PAUCAR AND THE DONKEY MADE A PLAN.

They went to the green hills. When they got to the cave where the old fox lived, the donkey stopped. Paucar pushed and shoved the donkey yelling, "Move you lazy thing!" But the donkey would not budge.

The foxes heard the shouts and came out. Suddenly the donkey let out a cry so terrible that Paucar ran away. Moaning, the donkey then fell to the ground. He rolled over on his back and lay as stiff as a board.

The foxes decided to cook the dead donkey for dinner. But they could not move him. Then the old fox remembered the ropes. She went into the cave and brought out all 20 ropes. The foxes began to tie the donkey up so they could pull him away. The donkey kept count of the ropes.

WHEN HE HAD COUNTED 20, HE JUMPED UP AND KICKED OUT IN ALL DIRECTIONS. THE FOXES WERE SO FRIGHTENED, THEY RAN FOR THEIR LIVES, DISAPPEARING FROM THAT REGION FOREVER.

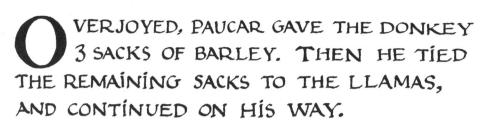

OVERJOYED, PAUCAR GAVE THE DONKEY
3 SACKS OF BARLEY. THEN HE TIED
THE REMAINING SACKS TO THE LLAMAS,
AND CONTINUED ON HIS WAY.

He could see Kanta below and hear the music of the quenas, guitars, and Indian harps.

chincheros, cuzco 1974
urcos

PAUCAR HAD NEVER SEEN SO MANY PEOPLE BEFORE!

He opened the sacks to show off his beautiful barley. Soon he had exchanged the barley for sweet potatoes, corn and quinua, a grain to make soup with. By noon, he had only a few sacks left. These he gave to an old man in exchange for a calf. Paucar was pleased. Now he and grandmother would have fresh milk and cheese to eat. Paucar had had a good day. He bought a tunic and a silver pin for grandmother, and set off for home.

GRANDMOTHER CRIED TEARS OF HAPPINESS WHEN SHE SAW HIM.

"YOU ARE A NOBLE DESCENDANT OF THE INCAS. YOUR MOTHER AND FATHER WOULD BE PROUD OF YOU," SHE SAID.

HER WORDS MADE PAUCAR HAPPY. HE GAVE HER THE PRESENTS HE HAD BROUGHT HER AND TOLD HER ABOUT HIS ADVENTURES.

After dinner Paucar looked out at the night and whispered "Thank you Mamita, thank you Papito. I miss you!" Then speaking to the hills he said, "Thank you Mama Pacha."

Glad to be at home, he went to bed. As he slept, the beautiful Andes stood watch over the night.